Kode's Quest(ion)

A Story of Respect

the Seven Teachings Stories

Katherena Vermette

Illustrated by Irene Kuziw

HIGHWATER
PRESS

Betsy, the cultural teacher, tells
Mashkode-Bizhiki (Kode for short)
that the next teaching is Respect.
Kode has heard that word before,
but she doesn't think she
knows what it means.

So, she asks the smartest
man she knows.
"What is respect, Nidede?"
Her dad tells her,
"Respect is when we treat
Mother Earth well."

Kode knows how to
be good to the earth.
She cleans up the yard
and rakes the leaves,
but she is still confused.

So, she asks the smartest
woman she knows.
"What is respect, Nimaamaa?"
Her mom tells her,
"Respect is when you are
good to people."

Kode knows how to do that.
She is kind to her classmates
and family,

but she is even more
confused about what
respect means.

So, she asks the smartest girl she knows.
"What is respect, Nimise?"
Her older sister tells her, "Respect is
when you honour your elders."

Kode knows how to do that.
She visits Gookom and Mishoom
and helps with their chores,
but she is even more confused than
ever about this word *respect*.

So, she asks the smartest boy she knows.
"What is respect, Nisaye?"
Her older brother tells her, "Respect is when you
are good to yourself in a good way."

I can do that, Kode thinks,
and that night she eats all her vegetables
because they are good for her,
but she is still confused.
How can respect mean so many things?

She has to ask the smartest old man she knows.
"What is respect, Nimishoomis?"
Her grandfather tells her,
"Respect is when you know and
live by the Seven Teachings."

Kode knows all the teachings:

Love
Bravery
Humility
Wisdom
Honesty
Truth
and Respect

Her head is full
of all of these things.

She has to talk to the smartest
old woman she knows.
"What does respect mean, Nookoomis?"
Her grandmother looks at her for a long time,
and says, "Respect is when you do the best
you can as much as you can."

Kode thinks about this for a long time.
She doesn't think she knows any more
than she did when she started.

She goes back to Betsy.
"Teacher, I asked my whole family,
but I don't think I know
what respect *means*."

"Oh?" says Betsy.

"What do you think it could mean?"

Kode takes a deep breath.
"It's something about being good to
the earth and your people, honouring
your elders and yourself in a good way,
and doing the best you can."

Betsy just smiles,

and Kode understands.